Silent Sam

written by Tabatha Jean D'Agata

illustrated by Geraldo Valério

Bebop Books

An imprint of LEE & LOW BOOKS Inc.

Gus has a parrot.
The parrot's name is Sam.
Gus wants to teach Sam to talk.

"Say Gus," Gus says to Sam.
Sam is silent.

5

Gus makes a tape.
He says, "Gus, Gus, Gus . . ."
until the tape ends.

Gus plays the tape for Sam.
Sam is silent.

Gus sings his name for Sam.
Gus cheers his name for Sam.

11

Gus even shouts his name.
But Sam is silent.

13

"Sam, you are no fun," Gus says.
Gus decides to play ball.

15

Gus kicks his ball.
The ball knocks over the plant.
"Oh no!" Gus says.

Mom rushes into the room.
She looks at the dirt on the floor.
"Who knocked over the plant?"
Mom asks.

19

Mom looks at Gus.
Gus looks at Sam.

"Gus, Gus, Gus," says Sam.

Gus has a parrot.
The parrot's name is Sam.
Gus wants to teach Sam
to be silent.